Dear Parents and Educators,

Welcome to Penguin Young Readers! As parents and educators, you know that each child develops at his or her own pace—in terms of speech, critical thinking, and, of course, reading. Penguin Young Readers recognizes this fact. As a result, each Penguin Young Readers book is assigned a traditional easy-to-read level (1–4) as well as a Guided Reading Level (A–P). Both of these systems will help you choose the right book for your child. Please refer to the back of each book for specific leveling information. Penguin Young Readers features esteemed authors and illustrators, stories about favorite characters, fascinating nonfiction, and more!

Max & Ruby: Max's Half Birthday

LEVEL **2**

GUIDED READING LEVEL **F**

This book is perfect for a **Progressing Reader** who:
- can figure out unknown words by using picture and context clues;
- can recognize beginning, middle, and ending sounds;
- can make and confirm predictions about what will happen in the text; and
- can distinguish between fiction and nonfiction.

Here are some **activities** you can do during and after reading this book:
- Word Repetition: Reread the story and count how many times you read the following words: *birthday, cake, gift, half, happy, party, thank, you.*
- Make Connections: In this story, Max has a half birthday party. If you had a half birthday party, how would you celebrate? Draw a picture of the invitations you would send.

Remember, sharing the love of reading with a child is the best gift you can give!

—Sarah Fabiny, Editorial Director
Penguin Young Readers program

*Penguin Young Readers are leveled by independent reviewers applying the standards developed by Irene Fountas and Gay Su Pinnell in *Matching Books to Readers: Using Leveled Books in Guided Reading*, Heinemann, 1999.

PENGUIN YOUNG READERS
An Imprint of Penguin Random House LLC

Cover art by Rosemary Wells

Library of Congress Cataloging-in-Publication Data is available.

ISBN 9780515157468 (pbk)   10 9 8 7 6 5 4 3 2 1
ISBN 9780515157475 (hc)   10 9 8 7 6 5 4 3 2 1

Max & Ruby!

Max's Half Birthday

by Rosemary Wells
illustrated by Andrew Grey

Penguin Young Readers
An Imprint of Penguin Random House

Max likes birthday parties.

Lily has a birthday party today.

Lily is four.

Max goes to her party.

Lily's mom makes a cake.

Lily's cake has four candles.

It has pink roses on top.

Max sings "Happy Birthday

to You"!

Max gives Lily a gift.

His gift is a set of fangs.

Lily likes the fangs very much.

She puts on the fangs.

"Thank you, Max," says Lily.

Jose has a birthday party, too.

Jose is five.

Jose's mom makes

ice-cream sodas.

Max gives Jose a gift.

His gift is a ball.

"Thank you, Max," says Jose.

They all play catch.

Now Max wants a birthday.

"No, Max," says his sister, Ruby.

"It is not your birthday."

"No fair!" says Max.

Max wants a birthday now.

Max wants a party now.

19

He wants a cake.

He wants gifts.

Max tells Grandma he wants a birthday now.

"Max," says Ruby,

"you are not four.

You are not five.

You are three and a half."

"Well, Max," says Grandma.

"You are not four.

You are not five.

But you can have

a half birthday party!"

Grandma makes cupcakes.

Ruby makes paper hats.

Ruby asks all her dolls
to come to the party.
Max asks all his robots
to come to the party.

Max puts on half of a shirt.

He puts on half of a paper hat.

29

Max has half of a cupcake.

All the dolls and robots sing

"Happy Half Birthday to You"!

Max goes to bed very happy.

He sings "Happy Half Birthday

to Max."

He falls asleep

still wearing his paper hat.